Book Level: 5.0

Points: 7.0

Quiz#: 166361

The Dominion Key

Also by Lee Bacon

The JOSHUA DREAD Series

Joshua Dread
Joshua Dread: The Nameless Hero

A Mutant Named Mizzie
(A Digital Original Short Story)